Introduction

Have you ever seen a mermaid? It is not surprising if you haven't, for they are very shy and hard to spot. It is much easier if you know what to look for.

First of all, you must be beside the sea, far away from cities and crowds. Then you must look at the place where the sea meets the sky and try not to think of anything at all.

There! Did you *almost* see a flash of silver on the water? Did you *nearly* spot a flash of golden mermaid hair? Did you *not quite* see the sparkle of a mermaid's smile? You did? Then you have seen as much of a mermaid as anyone has ever seen, and you are very, very lucky!

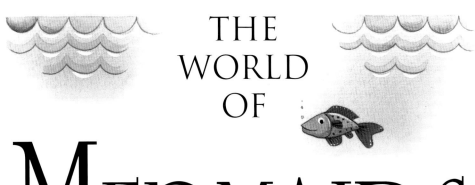

THE WORLD OF MERMAIDS

WRITTEN BY NICOLA BAXTER

ILLUSTRATED BY CATHIE SHUTTLEWORTH

ARMADILLO

Published by Armadillo Books
an imprint of
Bookmart Limited
Registered Number 2372865
Trading as Bookmart Limited
Desford Road Enderby
Leicester LE9 5AD
Exclusive to Chapters in Canada

ISBN 1-90046-632-5

Produced for Bookmart Limited by Nicola Baxter
PO Box 71 Diss Norfolk IP22 2DT
Editorial consultant: Ronne Randall
Designer: Amanda Hawkes

Printed in Singapore

Contents

A Mermaid's Special Wish

Far below the stormy sea, there is a wonderful watery world. There tiny fish of silver, jade and gold dart between pillars of pink and orange coral. Mermaids and mermen swim and sing, filling their sparkling cities with music. Everywhere you look there is something lovely. The paths are lined with gleaming pearls and shining shells. Seaweed gracefully sways beside the buildings, higher than trees on earth. Curious creatures peek from the sandy sea-floor, watching as the mermaids comb their gleaming hair.

It was in the mer-city of Corumbel that the mermaid of this story lived. She was called Ondine, and she was as beautiful as any mermaid you have ever seen. Her hair was not brown, or gold, or red. It shimmered like the sea itself—sometimes blue, sometimes green, sometimes lilac. And when the last rays of the setting sun flashed down through the water, it was the fierce orange of fire.

When Ondine was a baby, she made friends with a porpoise named Adolphus. Like her, he could breathe air but swim for a long time beneath the waves. She would hold on tight to one of Adolphus's fins and shriek with joy as he swooshed through the water, carrying her first over and then under the turquoise sea. Ondine hoped that she and Adolphus could be together forever.

But there is a big difference between merpeople and porpoises. Mermaids like Ondine live for hundreds of years. In fact, some people say they live forever. Porpoises are like humans. They are always changing. One day, when the sun is sparkling on the water, they swim away into the blue ocean never to be seen again. Please don't think that they have gone completely. They live on in the hearts of their friends and the memories of everyone who loved them.

Ondine was still very young in mermaid years when Adolphus swam out into the great ocean. For a long time, she was very sad and sometimes angry, too.

It was during this time that Ondine's grandfather found her one day, sitting on a rock above the water and watching the clouds drift across the sky.

"What a beautiful day it is," sighed the merman. "How lucky you are, Ondine, to be able to breathe this salty air and watch this sunny sky."

"It doesn't look the same," said the little mermaid, "without my friend. I wish he was here."

"But he is here," smiled her grandfather. "Just look around you. He is in everything you see."

"I don't understand," said Ondine with a frown.

"Did Adolphus love the sea?" asked her grandfather. "Did he like to leap into the sunshine and splash in the waves? Did he smile when he saw a rainbow in the sky? Did he laugh when you chased him through the blue water? Did he teach you to love all the things that he loved too?"

"Of course he did," said Ondine. "That's why I miss him so much. Whenever I see any of those things, it reminds me of him. I *do* wish he was here."

"That is a very special wish," her grandfather replied, "but do you really believe that Adolphus would want you to be unhappy when you see those things? He loved them. Now he is part of them all. He gave you a great gift by teaching you to love them too."

Ondine sighed. "I suppose I am lucky," she said. "And I was lucky to know Adolphus. But still, I wish…."

"Well," her grandfather smiled. "What do you usually do when you make a wish?"

"I touch my mermaid necklace, of course," said Ondine, putting her hand to where the little golden seahorse glittered around her neck. "It always makes my wishes come true. Oh! Do you really think I could wish Adolphus back?"

"It isn't what I think that matters," the old merman replied. "It is what you think that is important now. A special wish should not be made in a hurry. Why don't you think about it for a while? I will meet you here tomorrow to see what you have decided. Take care, my dear!"

With a flick of his silvery tail, the merman slipped beneath the waves.

Later that day, Ondine sat among the coral near her home and dangled her seahorse necklace from her fingers. It was a very special necklace, given to her when she was born. Every mermaid has one piece of jewelry—a brooch, a bracelet, a necklace, or an ornament for her hair—that is very special to her. Whenever she needs to think about something  important or to make a serious decision, she holds it in her hand. If the sea is stormy and she cannot sleep at night, she puts it under her pillow. When she is far from home or not feeling well, she touches it and soon feels better. All mermaids take very great care of their special jewelry.

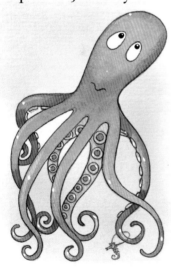 Ondine looked at the pretty necklace. Then she started to think about Adolphus. As she did so, she felt a sudden tug at her fingers and looked down. To her horror, she saw that her necklace was gone. It took her a second longer to realize that a small octopus was speeding away through the water, clutching something shiny.

Many feelings whirled through Ondine. At first she simply felt shocked. She could not believe that her necklace had been stolen. Then she felt angry. How dare some eight-legged creature take what was hers? In another moment, a great feeling of sadness washed over her. She had lost Adolphus and now she had lost her most precious possession.

But Ondine was a brave little mermaid. Tossing back her shimmering hair, she set off after the octopus, determined to force him to give back her necklace. He was so far ahead now that she could hardly see him.

Now, octopuses can swim very quickly. Ondine soon began to feel that she would never catch him. Suddenly, she remembered Adolphus speeding through the waves. He pushed hard with his powerful tail to move faster. Ondine swished her own tail in the water and found she could swim more quickly. "Thank you, Adolphus," she whispered.

Gradually, Ondine began to gain on the octopus. Closer and closer she swam, until she could almost stretch out her hand and reach his tentacles. Just as she thought she could grab him, he swam into a deep, dark cave.

Ondine was not frightened of very much, but she really hated deep, dark caves. Her first thought was to swim straight out as quickly as she had swum in. She paused, letting her eyes become accustomed to the dim light. As she looked around, Adolphus came into her mind once more. She remembered a time when she was small and had been swept onto the rocks by an enormous wave. Not thinking at all of his own safety, Adolphus had followed her, although he had always been afraid of being scraped and bruised by the sharp rocks. He had not given a thought to his fear when someone he loved was in danger.

Ondine shook her head. She too could be brave. Moving gently forward, she swam further into the dark cave and rounded a rocky corner.

In the next moment, she was almost dazzled by a brilliant light, flashing and dancing on a thousand sparkling jewels. The octopus had filled his home with pretty things that shimmered in the water. He sat in the middle of them, guarding his stolen possessions.

Ondine looked hard at the octopus. The octopus stared
back. He looked more frightened than mean.

"You can't have it back," he said. "It's mine now."

"No, it isn't," said Ondine firmly, surprised by her own
courage. "It will always be mine. And every time you
look at it, you will know that you stole it. I don't know
how you can bear to live with so much unhappiness."

"Unhappiness?" gasped the octopus. "What do you
mean? These things make me very happy. They make my
horrid, dark cave bright and pretty. I couldn't bear to
live without these things. They are all that I have. No
one ever visits me here."

Suddenly, Ondine felt very sorry for the octopus.
"Don't you have a family," she asked, "and friends to
play with?"

"They have all gone away to a new cave, full of light,"
said the octopus. "But I was too frigh… I mean, I
decided not to go, so I am here all alone, with all my
pretty things."

Ondine thought of her own life. She had relatives who
loved her. She had friends who cared about her. She had
a lovely home to live in and the whole wonderful ocean
to explore. She was very lucky. She remembered what
her grandfather had said to her and knew at once what
she had to do.

"I once lost a friend I loved very much," she said. "And I was afraid to be happy again because I thought it would mean I had forgotten him. But you cannot hold on to things that are gone. Everything changes, and we must change too. You can keep my necklace if it will make you happy, but I don't think it really will. Let me be your friend instead."

The octopus flushed a dull pink. "I'm safe in my cave," he said. "What will happen if I make friends outside? I might lose everything I have."

"The world outside is a wide and wonderful place," smiled Ondine. "Instead of living with memories of the unhappiness of so many mermaids you have stolen from, you could live with the happiness of real friends. Isn't it worth coming to find out?" And she stretched out her hands toward the sad little creature in his cave of jewels.

Nowadays, you would not recognize the little octopus. When he returned the jewels to their owners, the mermaids were so happy that they forgot to be angry with him. Now he has to swim faster than ever to find enough time to visit all of his friends.

Ondine is happy, too. Her golden seahorse hangs around her neck once more, but she has not used it to wish Adolphus back. She knows that he is part of her now. Because she once had a wonderful friend, she can make other wonderful friends. She knows that Adolphus would not want her to be sad.

And sometimes, when a certain funny little octopus whizzes past on his happy way, she thinks he even looks a little like a porpoise—when he smiles.

Amazing Mermaids

Mermaids, as you know, are very shy where humans are concerned. In spite of this, many stories and rhymes have been written about mermaids.

Perhaps the most famous of all is the Little Mermaid in the story by Hans Christian Andersen. He was the son of a poor Danish shoemaker but he always wanted to be a writer. Although he also wrote for grown-ups, today it is his fairy tales for children that are best remembered. The Danish people were so proud of him that they put up a statue to remind people of his wonderful stories. And what did they choose? A statue of the Little Mermaid, of course, placed next to the sea.

In the days of Queen Elizabeth I of England, a poet called Edmund Spenser wrote many verses in praise of her. The Queen's great rival was Mary, Queen of Scots. When the poet wanted to praise her too, he did it in a kind of code:

> ...once I sat upon a promontory
> And heard a mermaid on a dolphin's back
> Uttering such dulcet and harmonious breath,
> That the rude sea grew civil at her song;
> And certain stars shot madly from their spheres,
> To hear the sea-maid's music.

The mermaid was Mary. The dolphin was mentioned because Mary married the Dolphin (or Dauphin) of France, the French King's eldest son.

Alfred, Lord Tennyson described the kind of mermaid we all imagine. Would you like to be a mermaid?

> Who would be
> A mermaid fair,
> Singing alone,
> Combing her hair
> Under the sea,
> In a golden curl
> With a comb of pearl,
> On a throne?

Mermaid Secrets

Mermaids know more about the sea than anyone. Here are some magical mermaid secrets for you to look out for next time you are at the beach.

Fierce Flowers

Some of the flowers that surround a mermaid's palace are not plants at all. Beautiful sea anemones appear in many different shades but they are really animals. When a small fish or shrimp swims past, the petal-like tentacles pull it into a mouth in the middle of the false flower.

Mermaids' Purses

After a storm, the beach may be littered with little rectangular cases with pointed corners. These black, brown or pale yellow objects are often called mermaids' purses. In fact, they are the empty egg cases of dogfish and other fish. The pointed corners once ended in long tendrils that attached the egg case to seaweed. When the young fish hatch, they swim out of the egg case and leave it behind.

Sea Songs

Beaches are wonderful places to find shells. They may be long, thin razor-shells, wide, flat scallop shells or twisted, cone-shaped shells that are homes to whelks and other sea snails. If a shell is tightly closed, its owner is still inside and you should leave it alone, but empty shells are beautiful to collect. Large, twisted shells are special. If you hold them to your ear, you can hear the sound of the sea—and maybe a mermaid singing.

Mermaid Jewels

Every mermaid loves to wear jewels made from the treasures of the sea. You can make some more to wear with your special golden seahorse necklace.

Sea Shell Brooches

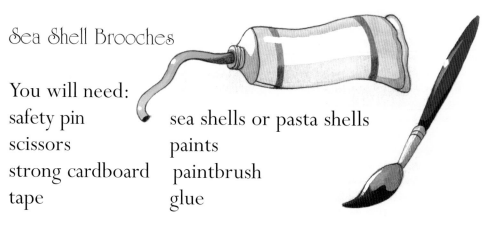

You will need:
safety pin   sea shells or pasta shells
scissors   paints
strong cardboard   paintbrush
tape   glue

1. Cut a piece of cardboard the size and shape you want your brooch to be. Carefully tape one side of a safety pin to the underside of the card. You don't need to open the pin.

2. Paint the cardboard and the pasta shells if you are using them. They can be as bright as you like—mermaids love the rainbow shades of the sea.

3. Arrange the shells or pasta shells on the front of the cardboard in any way you like, and glue them in place. You can paint or spray them with varnish or clear nail polish if you like.

Bracelets and Boxes

Tie short lengths of ribbon along a cord to make an anemone bracelet. Make a shell-covered box to put your jewels in.

Your Mermaid Name

A mermaid should have a beautiful name. Ondine means *wave*. Perhaps you need a special mermaid name, too. All the names on the next page are suitable for mermaids. Why not let your golden seahorse choose one for you?

All you have to do is to dangle your necklace above the page and swing it gently around and around. Then close your eyes and let the seahorse drop onto the page. The name nearest his nose is the name he has chosen for you! I hope you like it!

 Your Mermaid Name

Serena

Lorelei

Maris

Amber

Meredith

Aqua

Alcina

Hallie

Margaret

Coraline

Coral

Ariel

Undine

Selina

Naida

Nerissa

Seasprite

Marguerite

Aquaria

Marina

Meriel

Neptuna

Sirena

Oceana

Atlanta

Rosemary

Marissa

Starfish

Pearl